STORYBOOK

All in a Day's Work

MW00891217

Story by Holly Schroeder
Illustrations by Vicki Scott and Animated Arts

McGraw-Hill
Children's Publishing

A Division of The McGraw-Hill Companies

LANDOLL

Copyright © 2001 McGraw-Hill Children's Publishing. Published by Landoll, an imprint of McGraw-Hill Children's
Publishing, a division of The McGraw-Hill Companies.
Send all inquiries to:
McGraw-Hill Children's Publishing
8787 Orion Place
Columbus, Ohio 43240-4027

Bugs Bunny was in the middle of a very good dream . . .

. . . when the phone rang. It was the great Leopold Von Hickey, who was directing Bugs's latest picture.

"Bugs—quick! Like a bunny! Get down to the studio," Von Hickey barked.
"On my day off?" Bugs groaned.
"You had a day off last year!" the director replied. "Make like ze bunny and hop!"

"I'm gonna be so clean I'll squeak."

"Eh, let me see," Bugs said, "what costume should I wear today? I hope it's not a disaster movie, or anything with dinosaurs or little bald guys. . . ."

"Let's see—hmmm, little Tommy Nusseldorfer from Baltimore wants an autographed picture, Lilly O. deVallee wants a letter, and the gas company wants fifteen bucks! Some fan mail."

"Okay," said Von Hickey, "the first scene's a pie throw. Then, it's a boulder slam. After that you get blasted out of a cannon. Then, there's a 300-foot dive onto a wet sponge. But the fourth scene's pretty dangerous, so we'll use a stunt man."

"Eh, excuse me, Doc, but . . ."
"Quiet on the set! Lights! Camera! Action!!!"

"Cut! Is this coconut cream?" asked the director. "I wanted lemon meringue! Somebody get me another pie! And get the right one this time!"

"Cut!" shouted the director again. "You call that action? You call that pebble a boulder? Now, let's try that shot again!"

The crew was quiet. The director was thinking. A long time passed. "You know what will make this movie better?" he finally said brightly. "A bigger boulder!"

"You realize, of course, this means war."

The director wanted Bugs to do a dangerous stunt. "You will be shot from a cannon—but I promise, it will hurt me more than it hurts you. Now, let me think . . ."

"Let me help ya, Doc," said Bugs, grabbing a mallet from the prop table.

"Whattya know, Doc?! I think you were right! Now, step right
up in here and have a seat, and I'll be right wit'cha."

"Oh, this is gonna be a great picture!" Bugs said. "You're already seein' stars! Quick! You've gotta get cleaned up for the next scene."

Bugs helped the director up a tall ladder. "C'mon, c'mon, Leopold—move it! We haven't got all day!"

Bugs handed Von Hickey a bath towel and some soap. "Here ya go, Von Stinkelberg. Now, get down there and have yourself a nice sponge bath, after you dive into the sponge, that is."

"There!" said Bugs. "Don'tcha feel better?" Bugs was in a hurry. "Let's get movin'! One more appointment—for a shave and a haircut!"

"Another second and you'll be the perfect height," Bugs said.
"Wait!" yelled Von Hickey. "I'll go easier on you! I promise!"

"Eh, don't forget to write!" Bugs hollered. "Oh well, another day—another troublemaker." Then, there was a loud CRASH!

"Whattya know!" said Bugs. "I've been in this business for awhile—you'd think I'd know scenery when I see it. Oh, well, all in a day's work!"